STRAWBERRIES IN THE SEA

BOOKS BY ELISABETH OGILVIE

*Available from Down East Books

Bennett's Island Novels

The Tide Trilogy
  High Tide at Noon*
  Storm Tide*
  The Ebbing Tide*

The Lovers Trilogy
  The Dawning of the Day*
  The Seasons Hereafter*
  Strawberries in the Sea*

An Answer in the Tide*
The Summer of the Osprey
The Day Before Winter*

Children's Books

The Pigeon Pair
Masquerade at Sea House
Ceiling of Amber
Turn Around Twice
Becky's Island
How Wide the Heart
Blueberry Summer
Whistle for a Wind
The Fabulous Year
The Young Islanders
Come Aboard and Bring
  Your Dory!

Other Titles

My World is an Island*
The Dreaming Swimmer
Where the Lost Aprils Are
Image of a Lover
Weep and Know Why
A Theme for Reason
The Face of Innocence
Bellwood
Waters on a Starry Night
There May be Heaven
Call Home the Heart
The Witch Door
Rowan Head
No Evil Angel
A Dancer in Yellow
The Devil in Tartan
The Silent Ones
The Road to Nowhere
When the Music Stopped

The Jennie Trilogy
  Jennie About to Be*
  The World of Jennie G.*
  Jennie Glenroy*